A big thank you to the hundreds of kids I met
on school visits who helped me with ideas
for these books!

# Jenny Oldfield

# my little life

## When Dad went on a Date

illustrated by Martina Farrow

Hodder
Children's
Books

a division of Hodder Headline Limited

Text copyright © 2002 Jenny Oldfield
Illustrations copyright © 2002 Martina Farrow
Cover illustration © 2002 Nila Aye

First published in Great Britain in 2002
by Hodder Children's Books

A Catalogue record for this book is available from the British Library

ISBN 0 340 85075 2

Printed and bound in Great Britain by
Bookmarque Ltd, Croydon, Surrey

Hodder Children's Books
A division of Hodder Headline Limited
338 Euston Road, London NW1 3BH

# Wednesday, January 31st

We can't afford to eat. It's official.

Dad has to pay a monster gas and electricity bill. Scott clocked up a record £180 yakking non-stop to friends on their mobiles. Bud just cost us £75 for infected ears (vet plus medicine, all because of some microscopic mites. Poor Bud practically went mental. So did Dad when he paid the fee). On top of which, we still haven't got over Christmas.

I don't get it. You spend loads of dosh on pressies, cards, wrapping, lights, Chrissy trees, partying, nosh etcetera, then it takes you half a year to recover. Since when did Christmas and baby Jesus turn into a disease?

Anyway, according to Dad, we haven't got over it yet.

'I have five customers owing me for work I did last November,' he mutters, stacking the unpaid bills behind the clock. 'The van needs an MOT, Scott wants new trainers, and Gina's late with her maintenance payment.'

I'm frowning. I open an envelope with a free CD inside. I find out I didn't win the DVD player I wanted when I entered the competition; only the freebie CD by some group I've never even heard of. Scott leans over my shoulder and grabs it. 'Give it here.'

I hang on tight. 'No. What for?'

'I'll flog it at school. We'll go fifty-fifty.'

'Yeah, whatever.' I let go and return to my soggy cornflakes. 'These are stale!' I wail at Dad.

'Yeah, well get used to it, Tiff,' he grunts. 'Food is way down the bottom of my list of priorities this month. We'll have to scrape by on what we've got in the house.'

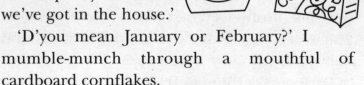

'D'you mean January or February?' I mumble-munch through a mouthful of cardboard cornflakes.

Dad glances at the cat calendar Mum gave us for Christmas. ('You lot will never keep yourselves organised without one!')

'February, of course.'

'You mean, we gotta starve for four whole weeks!' Scott howls.

Dad shrugs. Business is bad. The bills are stacking up. What can he do?

School's boring. B-O-R-I-N-G.

I'm supposed to be doing a sketch of my own hand or foot for art homework, only I left my sketch-book in the art room. That leaves time to work on my short story for the competition that Mr Fox 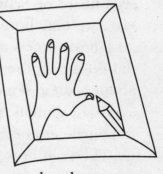 told us about – so far there are two brothers, one kills the other, seals up body inside thick stone wall of house they've been building together. Dead brother haunts house with ghostly voice, but no one can find his body in the hidden tomb. The voice cries out for vengeance and drives people mad all through the centuries right up to the present day . . .

Decide I don't like it after all.

Bummer. Nothing's going right. Will have to start all over again.

Down in dumps. Grotty. Grungy. Narked off!

'What's that face for?' Mum asked half an hour ago. She called to collect Dad in her silver Ka (2 years old, 18,000 miles, chosen by Neil). The pair of them (Mum and Dad, that is) were making a huge effort to go along to my parents' evening together, to let the school know that getting divorced and Mum going off with Neil didn't mean they'd suddenly stopped caring about Scott and me.

What I think is, they don't need to try so hard to convince other people. I know they still love us. They can go separately to parents' evenings from now on, for all I care. I mean, it definitely doesn't bother me!!! Like, yeah.

So, 'What's that face?' from Mum didn't go down too well.

'Are you having a tough time, Tiff?'

'No!'

'You sure?' Dad was upstairs getting changed out of his work clothes. The shower was running, he was clumping about. Mum glanced at her watch. 'You look as if something's bothering you.'

10

'I'm bored!'

'Is that all?' She gave me The Look = 'You can tell me, I'm your Mum!'

'Yeah. School's boring. Scott's boring. Telly's boring!'

'Go round to Ellie's or Geri's.'

'Nah.'

'Ring Fuchsia.'

'Nah.'

'Well *do* something. Don't sit around looking like a wet weekend.'

Thanks for the sympathy, Mum!

Dad came down looking cool. He scrubs up good when he gets the plaster dust off. His hair's still really dark and thick, he's got smiley eyes and one of those dimples in his chin. Mum looked cool too, in her grey work trouser suit and white roll-neck sweater.

'Ross, Tiffany's bored!' Mum announced. 'Can't you find her a job?'

Thanks again, Mum!

'Yeah. Wash up, walk the dog, hoover the front room, tidy your bedroom . . .'

I told him I'd got tons of homework and flounced out.

'It's Scott's turn to take Bud for a walk!' I yelled from halfway up the stairs. Half-asleep on the landing, Bud heard his name, leaped up and shot downstairs. I stepped smartly to one side, and the daft mutt did a somersault down the rest of the stairs into the hallway, picked himself up and pounced on Mum – lick-lick!

'Down!' Her suit was suffering. He was tugging the cuff, slavering over her. Finally she broke free. 'Bye, Tiffany! Bye, Scott!' she called out over the barks and yelps.

'Bye!'

'Bye!'

'And don't fight, you two!' Dad warned before he closed the front door.

Yeah. And I'm Britney Spears!!!

# Saturday, 3rd February

***Your stars*** *– Leo girls need to sparkle. Get out the body glitter and boogie along to your fave CD. Invite your mates to make it all worthwhile.*

```
BORED    B    B    BORING
O        E    O O  SNORING
R        R    R    IGNORING
E        O    E E  POURING
DEROB    D    D    ROARING
```

No new ideas for short story. Writers' block. Sigh, groan.

Thursday (day before yesterday), handed in my hand (Ha ha!).

Ellie away for weekend.

Geri playing hockey.

Shah grounded (Her mum and dad say she can't go out until she's caught up on all her coursework. Miss Hornby dobbed her in on Wednesday night. 'Of course, we all love Fuchsia to bits because she's so sweet-natured, talented and unusual. But she'll find that eccentricity per se won't get her very far in life without the necessary hard work to accompany it. Not to put too fine a point on it, Mr and Mrs Allerton, your daughter is simply not doing any work!')

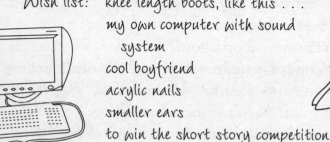

Wish list:  knee length boots, like this . . .
my own computer with sound
     system
cool boyfriend
acrylic nails
smaller ears
to win the short story competition

Fat chance. The ear thing is bugging me. I can cover them with my hair, but then I can't wear interesting styles with scrunchies and clips. And if the wind blows my hair back from my face, I always think Chucky or Squealer or Dom Skinner is gonna yell 'Dumbo!' at me and start flapping their ears.

It's not a joke, it's serious having part of your anatomy you're ashamed of. And let's not get into bra sizes (Still 30AA and vanishing!)

Wow, how sad is that? Have just re-read today. Bummer!!!

Mum rang.

'Hi, Tiff, I thought I'd catch up with a quick chat. What're you up to?'

'Hi. Nothing.'

'Listen, do I have a superstar daughter, or what?'

'What're you on about?'

'Wednesday night, of course. All your teachers said you were settling in brilliantly and doing really well. Didn't your dad tell you?'

'Kind of.' Dad had come home smiling, at least.

'Mr White said you were his best pupil!'

'Which Mr White? Maths or Geography?'

'Geography. Maths Mr White also said he was very pleased with your progress.'

If you ask me, Maths Mr White doesn't even know who I am. Tiffany Little; a name on a list. Still, all this was suddenly making me feel much better.

'And Mr Fox thinks you have a special talent for writing.' Gorgeous George, my favourite teacher.

'Did he actually say that?'

A SPECIAL TALENT
FOR WRITING!

'Yes, word for word, I swear. And he asked where you got it from, and we laughed and said we didn't know, because neither your dad nor I have an ounce of creativity in us! . . . Tiff?'

'Yeah, I'm still here.' Wow, I have a special talent! Georgeous has seen my poems and stories, and he must know what he's talking about. He's read Shakespeare and stuff.

'Well, I'm really proud of you, honey.' Mum's voice broke up a bit at this point. 'Your dad and me; we both are.'

I felt I ought to be choked up too, but the funny thing was, I wasn't.

*p.m.*

Big Mac and fries for lunch.

Told Dad Mum rang about parents' evening. He said yeah, they'd both come out grinning from ear to ear. 'The only one Gina didn't get along with was Miss Ga . . . Miss Gu . . . the art teacher.'

'Ganeri. She's cool.'

'A bit too wacky for your mum, going on about

16

self-expression through art and how art can be good therapy, and all that. As far as Gina's concerned, art is about painting pretty sunflowers, full stop.'

'Miss Ganeri just gave me an A+ for my hand.'

Dad raised his eyebrow, but didn't ask. 'Here's a fiver.' He slipped the note into my pocket.

'Oh no, Dad, you don't have to . . .' I said without meaning it, but I felt I ought to because he's got all these bills to pay.

'Don't argue,' he told me. 'Go and get your Big Mac.'

Oh, and Mum's gonna buy me some boots in the mid-season Sales. Next weekend.

'With heels?' I asked over the phone. Catch her in a good mood.

'Not too high,' she agreed.

That's fine by me.

We've just been whacked by a whirlwind, tossed about by a tornado, hassled by a hurricane. In other words, Gran Little dropped by.

She lives thirty miles away, by the sea. My grandad died two years ago and Gran doesn't drive, but she doesn't let small things like having to catch three buses to our house stop her.

'Where's Ross? Where's my baby boy, Scott?' she demanded before I'd even opened the door to let her in.

Her baby boy, Scott, was glued to his computer. Dad had gone out on an afternoon job, but was due back any time.

Gran barged in and hugged me. She cooee-ed her way into the sitting room, then the kitchen. Bud jumped up and licked her face.

'Don't let him do that,' Scott grumped. He'd slopped down in his socks, with his baggy

 jeans hanging round his hips. 'Jumping up's a bad habit.'

'Bad habit-schmabit!' Gran laughed. She grappled with Bud and tweaked his ears. 'We're only having a bit of fun, aren't we, kiddo?' Then she grabbed Scott before he could escape, and did the same to him.

Kettle, tea-bags, milk, sugar, mugs. I went through the routine while my brother squirmed and hung on to his trousers.

'You're a walking skellington!' Gran cried, producing home-made choccy cake from her shopping bag.

(Gran's pet words — skellington
                     par cark
                     jim jams
                     kiddo)

She force-fed Scott and me the cake and gave big chunks to Bud. He drooled over the kitchen floor (Bud, not Scott. Though Scott does do some drooling when he's watching Buffy).

Then Dad came in and got the hugs and tweaks treatment.

Question: Did my ears get too big from Gran Little tweaking them when I was a baby? I mean, she's always been a tweaker, ever since I can remember. And it can't do a kid's ears any good, can it?

'And how are you, need I ask?' Gran had put Dad down and seized a damp cloth. She was rubbing sticky surfaces and wiping dribbles off cupboard doors. From the start, Gran had decided that Dad, Scott and me (I – me? I'm never gonna get that!!) couldn't manage without Mum.

19

'Fine,' Dad told her.

'You don't look fine,' Gran argued. 'You look worn out, working on Saturday afternoons, of all things. And Scott hasn't eaten a decent meal all week, I bet. What did you have for lunch, Scott? As for Tiffany, well why isn't she playing out with her friends in the fresh air, having a good time? The poor girl shouldn't be moping around the house at her age.'

Try telling Gran that at eleven going on twelve, playing out in the fresh air in early February when it's blowing a gale sounds like torture!

Gran is 61, going on 16. She believes in fresh air and high winds for people of all ages. 'Exercise!' She breathes in and flexes her biceps. 'Look what it does for me!'

We kid her about it. Dad says she'll be climbing Everest when she's 80. Last summer, she cycled across from the coast with a chocolate cake in her saddle-bag, stayed overnight then cycled back next day. She dyes her hair jet black and wears bright patterned leggings. She still buys Dad *The Beano*, rolls it up and sends it in the post.

She's mad. Stark staring. A complete nutter. But you wouldn't swap her for anyone else's gran in a million years.

And another thing about her – she never cares what she says or who hears it.

'Ross,' she said to my dad, after the kitchen was spotless and she'd rustled up bacon, eggs, beans and tomatoes for tea.

I'd arranged a face on my plate – two half-tomatoes for eyes, fried egg for a nose, bacon for the mouth and beans on top for the hair.

'Ross, I think it's time for you to persuade Gina to come back home!'

'Give it a rest, Mum, will you!' Dad concentrated on his crispy bacon, crunching it loudly. 'Pass the ketchup,' he said to Scott.

'Listen to me, I know what I'm talking about. What Gina's been having is a mid-life crisis. It happens all the time. And I remember myself what it's like when your babies are finally growing up and you're stuck in the house, cleaning and cooking all the time with no one so much as saying thank you.' Gran's voice had softened. 'A woman likes to feel appreciated, Ross.'

Dad slopped tomato sauce over his baked beans.

'When was the last time you bought Gina flowers, for instance? . . . Exactly! You see what I'm getting at. So she got to the point where she'd had enough, packed her bags and left the lot of you.

'She found herself a nice little flat and a steady job, stood on her own feet for the first time in her life. And I expect the experience has done her a lot of good.'

'You've talked to her lately, have you?' Dad mumbled.

'I don't need to talk to her to know how she's feeling. Gina's a good, kind girl, and I've always felt close to her. The moment you walked in on your Dad and me with her on your arm, what with that lovely auburn hair and wide smile – we took to her like ducks to water.'

'She's dyed it blonde – her hair,' Dad cut in again. But there was no stopping Super-Gran. 'But now Gina's had time to branch out on her own, and prove to herself she can do it. So she'll be getting home these dark nights, looking around her tidy little flat and wondering. She'll be realising what she's lost, that there was no reason to throw the baby out with the bath water as it were . . .'

Baby and bath water. What's that got to do with anything? Gran had paused for breath, and I got hung upon this small point. Baby and bath water. Hmm.

Dad shook his head. 'You're wrong there, Mum.'

'Nonsense. I know! And like I said, this is the right moment for you to make a move, Ross. Forget your differences, remind Gina of all the happy times you've had together; you, her, Scott and Tiffany. Convince her that it can be like that again, get her to come back home!'

Gran's voice had risen again. Listening to her, I could believe that it would all happen just the way she said.

Then Dad pushed his plate away and spoke. 'I don't think Neil would be very pleased about that.'

'Who's Neil?' Gran shot a glance across the table at Scott and me.

'You tell her,' Dad grunted at Scott.

'Mum's new boyfriend.'

That should have been it – end of painful conversation. But Gran's hand flew up in the air as if she was swatting a fly. 'Pooh, never mind about that! This Neil; what does he know? Gina's Gina, and she's not just going to fall into the arms of the first man who comes along!'

## Sunday, 4th February

*Your stars* – *A fun and funky peek into the future shows a sleepover towards the end of next week. Invite the frenz, order the pizza and milkshakes, dive out for a fave video and have a great night!*

Am considering magic as a subject for my short story. Wizards, witches, black cats.

'Get real!' Ellie said. 'Everyone's doing wizards these days. You need something completely different.'

Ellie thinks she knows everything. I sulked. But Geri agreed. 'Do a story about sport!' she yelled above the noise of the traffic. She'd dragged us across the road to look at trainers in the sports shop window. Fuchsia had nearly been run over by a bus. 'Y'know; a girl who's a high-jump star, with legs up to her ears, who's training for the next Olympics. Then she's in a car smash and hurts her leg. It looks like her dreams have been shattered. Her coach gives up on her, and everyone says she'll never make it into the UK Athletics team. But Aretha – that's her name – refuses to give up. She trains secretly, going through agony, getting her leg stronger day by day . . .'

We all stared at Geri. She was really into Aretha's story, so we let her finish.

Her eyes were glued to the most expensive pair of trainers in the window – anti-shock, high abrasion stitching, sculpted outersole. 'Nobody knows she's doing this, but she's determined to prove everyone wrong. There's only two days to go before they announce the final squad. It's the last athletics meeting before the selectors decide, the final jump-off between the two high-jumpers still left in the competition, and both of them have failed to jump the Olympic qualifying height.

'Suddenly, Aretha shows up out of the blue and all eyes in the stadium are on her. The crowd holds their breath as she measures her run-up to the bar. She gets ready, stands on tip-toe, then rests back and tests her injured leg. There's a sigh around the ground; no, she's not ready, the leg still hurts. But Aretha grits her teeth, she runs, she leaps up, flips on to her back, arches, kicks and clears the bar by half a metre!'

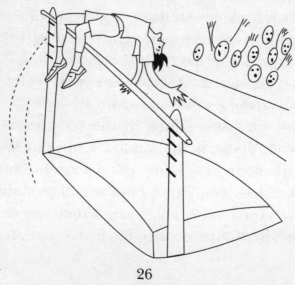

'The crowd goes mad!' Ellie breaks in. 'Aretha! Aretha! they chant.'

Then it's Shah's turn to interrupt. 'Aretha raises both arms towards them. She picks out her mum in the crowd – the only person in the world who believed she could do it – and Aretha jogs towards her. She takes a Union Jack flag from her mum and waves it above her head. She does a victory lap. She's crying and laughing at the same time. She's back in world class athletics – for good!'

'Hey, yeah!' Geri, Ellie and Shah sigh. 'What a great story. Tiff, you've gotta write it, and then we all get to share the prize!'

'You must be joking.' I'm tutting and tossing my head, like this is the most corny idea I've ever heard. Stick to whacking a hockey ball, Geri. Concentrate on the singing, Ellie. And Shah, well, just carry on being dreamy old you! Secretly I kicked myself for not thinking of it myself.

'I'd die for those trainers!' Geri switched subjects, thank heavens.

With the fiver Dad had given me in my pocket, I'm not thinking trainers. I'm thinking more sequin purse or wacky pair of socks with strawberries printed on.

Ellie soon got bored with sculpted outersoles. 'C'mon, let's go inside!' she moaned. 'I'm freezing out here.'

So we followed her into the shopping centre, telling jokes.

'What d'you get if you cross a snowman with a vampire?' Shah asked.

'We dunno. What d'you get?' I replied. Wait for it.

'Frostbite!'

'Aagh, no, that's so funny – NOT!!' Ellie wailed, dragging us towards Accessorize.

Go, Leo, go! There was enough glitter in here for a whole herd of us. Or should that be 'pride'? A pride of lions. I bought a funky red flat cap in the sales. Like this –

Geri bought a yellow coat-hanger with a squishy, smiley face stuck on. Shah chose Glitter-babe Lush Lip-gloss. For once Ellie didn't spend any money on anything. 'I'm saving up,' she murmured.

'What for?' we all demanded.

'Wait and see,' she smirked.

Weird. This is the first time in her life that Ellie

ever saved for anything! Her mum and dad are Mr and Mrs Millionaire. She asks and they buy. You'd think it would make her dead posh, which she is a bit, but not too bad really.

Anyway, after the bits and bobs shop, we hit the music store. We listened to a lot of Top Twenty stuff, but didn't buy. Saw Scott and Nic Heron in the distance. Scott turned his back as if he hadn't seen us, which everyone knew he had, but Nic came over to where we stood.

Nic could be a popstar himself, he's so cool. Not moody and mean like the rapsters, but cute and nice. His hazel eyes smile at you, his brown and blonde hair sticks straight up in streaked spikes, like a thick, stiff mop.

'Hey, Tiffany,' he said. 'I like the cap.'

My face turned crimson to mach the colour of my new hat.

'Hey, Ellie. Hey, Geri.' Then he turned to Fuchsia. 'Hey, Shah, have you heard from Skye lately?'

Since Christmas, when Shah's half-sister, Skye, came down from Scotland to spend time with her dad, Nic's made a big thing of asking Shah about Skye. You can't blame him – Skye's mega gorgeous model material. But it ruined my theory that Nic was interested in Shah. Yeah, OK, Shah's four years younger than Nic, but then again, Skye's three years older than him.

'Yeah, she e-mailed us on Wednesday,' Shah told him. 'She wants to come down and visit again at Easter.'

'Cool,' Nic said, looking mega-pleased.

'Do you want me to tell her you were asking?'

'Er – no thanks!' he muttered, like he'd been shot. He made a speed-demon exit through main door, with Scott tagging on behind.

Hmm. Either Nic's dead embarrassed about the idea of Skye finding out that he fancies her. Or else, it's not really Skye he's interested in, but Shah after all – and talking about Skye is just an excuse for him to get up close and personal. Which could it be? If you ask me, Nic's gonna wait a couple of years for Shah to turn into this drop-dead gorgeous babe. Then he's gonna move in on her, by which time he'll be a computer millionaire or a movie star . . .

'I gotta go,' I told the others as we stood watching Nic leave the store.

'Hey, you're sneaking away to catch up with Scott and Nic!' Ellie accused me. She'd give anything to be in Nic's crowd.

'I wish!' I sighed. My darling brother would boot me out if I even so much as hung around in Nic's shadow, quiet as a mouse, not saying anything, just drooling. 'Nah, I gotta meet my dad outside Top Shop.'

Geri made a surprised 'huh?' sound, then giggled.

'Yeah, I know,' I agreed. 'He wants to look in Top Man for a new jacket.'

The tittering passed on to Ellie and Shah.

'So what? He needs advice!' My own mouth began to twitch and a splutter came up from deep below. Soon we were all laughing and giggling. A woman gave us a dirty look. We fell about.

I mean, my dad buying clothes! My dad in a shop! My dad too scared to go in by himself – aah, bless!

'Anyway, I can't afford it,' he told me.

We'd met up as planned. He'd wanted to chicken out before we even got through the door. I'd lost him three times – once by the shirts, once amongst boxer shorts, and the third time he escaped while the assistant unlocked the security chain on the leather jackets. I'd dragged him back and made him try a couple on, but even I had to admit that he looked like one of those seedy dispatch riders who wear long ponytails and need a shave, who always turn out to be the baddies in episodes of *The Bill.* In the end, we'd given up and gone out into the precinct to look for a café.

I got a Coke and he bought a coffee. We squidged into the only free table in the place. Dad said sorry to a woman with her back to us whose shoulder he'd nudged.

She turned round and it was Miss Ganeri.

 'Oh hi, Tiffany!' she said with a bright smile. She was wearing a furry, purple and black sweater and her black hair had lots of tiny plaits with purple beads at the end. Purple nails and purple lip gloss, all colour co-ordinated, except for little tiny silver hooped earrings. 'Hi, Mr . . .'

'Ross,' he cut in, and then shook hands. Mr Smoothie.

'Hi, Ross. I'm Carli. I never expected the shopping centre to be this busy on a Sunday.'

'I know; nightmare,' Dad said.

'What did you buy?'

'Nothing, as it happens. I was looking for a jacket. How about you?'

'Nothing. I'm hopeless. I'm still trying to spend Christmas money that my parents gave me, but I can never find anything I like.'

OK, cut the chat! I gulped my Coke and looked at my watch. It was bad enough being seen shopping with Dad, but being caught talking to my art teacher out of school was even worse! I coughed and shuffled to attract Dad's attention to my empty can.

'Well, better get a move on,' he told Miss Ganeri. They'd already covered the evils of mindless shopping till you dropped, plus the latest top positions in the Premier League.

He got up and squeezed out of his corner. 'Nice seeing you, Carli.'

'Yes, and you, Ross. Take care, Tiffany. Bye.'

We got outside the café into the wide, glass-covered walkway. Phew, no one saw me!

'Talk about coincidence!' Dad muttered. 'I only meet the woman for the first time at parents' evening, and here we are bumping into her again in the middle of town!'

I gave him a quick look, then he changed the

subject. But I'd seen the way he was staring back into the café as we walked away, at Miss Ganeri in her fluffy purple sweater, with her big dark eyes and long eyelashes. And there was something in that look that turned on a light inside my head – bam! It hit me between the eyes.

Yeah, brilliant idea! I mean, a mega-fantastic, funky way of getting my dad out of the dumps he'd been in since Mum left home!!!

And I couldn't wait to let Shah, Geri and Ellie in on it. Still can't. And I know I'm not gonna get to sleep tonight for thinking about it!!!

## Monday, 5th February

*Your stars – You're over-excited at the moment, so make sure you take some time to chill out. Turn your bedroom into a haven of peace and tranquillity...*

Puh-lease!!!

'Well?' I asked.

It was 10.30a.m., break time. My eyes felt like hard-boiled eggs. I hadn't slept a wink.

'Well what?' Geri said, between mouthfuls of smoky bacon crisps.

'Well, isn't it cool?'

'What's cool?' Ellie looked like she hadn't listened to a word I'd said. She was gazing across B Hall at hunky Nic. 'D'you mean the way Nic Heron manages to wear his  school tie as if he's not wearing a uniform at all?' she said dreamily.

'Ignore her,' Shah advised. 'Yeah, Tiff, I think it's really cool that you care enough about your dad to fix up a date between him and Miss Ganeri!'

'Hmm-mmm-ufff!' Geri added. *Crunch-crunch-swallow.*

'Don't you think it'd be great?' I waved a hand across Ellie's face. 'My dad and Miss Ganeri!'

'How d'you know he fancies her?' she quizzed. 'Was he chatting her up?'

'Sort of.' If you can count discussing the Liverpool–Leeds match as chatting up.

'Your dad deserves something nice to happen,' Shah sighed.

How can you sort of chat somebody up?' Geri wanted to know. She blew air into her crisp bag, then popped it. Crisp crumbs showered over Ellie's shirt.

'Yuck, Geri, that's disgusting!' Ellie turned her back and drew me to one side. 'Listen, Tiff, I know your dad's a loser in lurve and all that . . .'

'Hang on, who are you calling a loser?' I stuck up for him before she could go on.

'Only in love,' she added. 'And no way was it his fault that your mum left. But are you sure this date thing will work out the way you want?'

'Yeah, course it will. It's fate!' I told them about us bumping into Miss Ganeri in the shopping centre.

'You mean, "Of all the cafés in all the world, she had to walk into this one!"?' Ellie drawled in an American accent.

'Right!' I didn't get the fact that she was sending me up until I thought about it later. 'You see; F-A-T-E!'

'OK, so how are you gonna make it happen?' Ellie got down to basics. 'I take it he didn't actually ask her out at the café?'

'No,' I frowned. 'But don't worry, I've thought

of a way. It involves mobile phones, and that's where you, Geri and Shah come in.'

'Hang on!' Geri pushed her nose in again. 'Did I hear my name?'

'We've got Art next, right?' The end-of-break bell was about to ring. I needed to get the plan in place fast. 'I want you three to distract Miss Ganeri while I creep to the front desk and sneak a look at her phone. You have to keep her long enough for me to find out the number and put the phone back as if I'd never touched it.'

'Phew!' Shah let out a long breath.

'Then what?' Geri asked. She was looking at me as if I'd completely lost it.

Then the bell went, and I didn't have time to explain.

'Oh, and by the way,' I dropped in as we shot upstairs to the Art Room, 'I'm having a sleepover on Saturday. Can you come?'

'Is your dad OK about having all three of us?' Shah asked.

He doesn't know yet.'

'Then how come you're inviting us?' Geri quizzed.

I swung through the door into a room littered with scribbly sketches, splodgy paintings, half-made plaster models and squidgy clay pots. 'Because it's in my stars!' I breezed. 'And Leo chicks are born to have FUN!'

I can always rely on Ellie, the drama queen.

'Miss, please Miss, Ellie's fainted!' Geri cried, and everyone in the Art Room looked round to see this figure zonked out on the floor.

Ellie's faint looked dead convincing. Her fair hair was swished out like a halo, her head to one side, her face pale. Miss G dropped what she was doing. She ran to Ellie's side and dropped down on to her knees. Chucky and Squealer led the rush to crowd around and gawp.

'Stand back!' Miss G ordered. 'Give her some air!'

But the mad crush helped me to sneak to the front without being seen.

'Miss, is she dead?' Squealer asked.

'Don't move her, Miss!' Chucky advised. 'Shall I call 999?'

'No, Chucky, stay where you are. Geri, what happened? Did she hit her head when she fell?'

Poor Miss G was still swamped by kids, so I fiddled with the mountain of papers on the front desk, trying to find her moby. I knew she kept it somewhere on the desk – not in her bag – but there was so much mess I couldn't find it.

'I didn't see her fall, Miss,' Geri sniffled, then mumbled something about hearing Ellie say she felt dizzy, but she didn't take much notice blah-de-blah.

I scrabbled around and finally grabbed the phone. Beep-beep – I started pressing buttons to find Own Number.

'Uuh-uuhh!' Ellie groaned.

'Huh, she's alive!' Squealer said in a disgusted voice.

'Uuuh, where am I? What happened?'

'Stand back, everyone!' Miss G insisted. 'Ellie, try to sit up and bend your head forward – that's it. Now, Fuchsia, open that window. Adam, I said stand well away, let Ellie breathe!'

I scribbled Miss Ganeri's number in biro on the palm of my hand. Gotcha!

'OK, panic over,' Miss G insisted. 'Geri will take Ellie to the Rest Room. The rest of you, get on with your work.'

So we all shuffled back to our places, mumbling.

Nice one, Ellie!

'What's up with you?' Chucky Gilbert muttered at me. 'Why are you grinning?'

'Nothing. I'm not. Shut up.'

'What were you doing with Miss G's phone?'

Nicked! And by the dumbest, clunkiest kid in the Year. Chucky thought so slowly you could hear his brain clicking and whirring. Which was lucky for me, really. 'I was gonna call an ambulance,' I lied.

Chucky thought about it. 'Yeah, good idea, Tiff,' he agreed. 'That's what I was gonna do.'

'What are you up to?' Scott wanted to know.

This was an hour ago, when Dad was in the shower and I was secretly texting a message on his phone:

Hi, Carli! Got your number frm a friend.
Enjoyed tlking yestdy, wd like to take u out.
How 'bout Wed? Meet u at Salvos, 7.30pm.
Ross Little

I hid the phone behind my back. 'Nothing, Scott. Get lost!'

'Let me see!' He made a grab and crashed into the kitchen table. Bud thought it was a game and started belting around the room barking.

I clicked the Send button, then switched the phone off. If Scott found out what I'd just done, I got the feeling he'd have a mega strop.

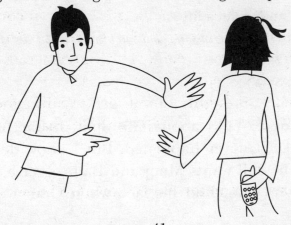

41

This is how it would go:

> *Me*:  Actually, as it happens, I just set Dad up on a date with our art teacher, Miss Ganeri.
>
> *Scott*: You must be joking!
>
> *Me*:  No, I'm serious.
>
> *Scott*: Are you off your *bleeping* head?!!! Does Dad know about this?
>
> *Me*:  Not yet. It's gonna be a surprise. Like a blind date.
>
> *Scott*: *Bleep-bleeping-bleep*! Who d'you think you are, Cilla *Bleeping* Black? Dad doesn't need you to set him up with any weirdo art teacher!
>
> *Me*:  Yes, he does. All he ever does is mope around this place. He needs to go out more, get a life.
>
> *Scott*: (*turning crimson, about to burst a blood vessel*) Says who?
>
> *Me*:  Says me!!!

Scott never talks about The Split. In fact, he acts like it never happened. But I know deep down he still wants Mum and Dad to get back together. I watched his face when Gran went on about it. So he would definitely disapprove of my little Cilla act.

'Kids, quit it, will you?' Dad bellowed from the top of the stairs.

Scott had me pinned against the cooker, which luckily wasn't on. I held the phone out of reach.

'Tiff's been using your phone!' big bro snitched.

Bud sprinted up and down stairs like a crazy thing.

Dad dripped his way down with a towel wrapped around his waist. 'When are you two gonna grow up?' he grumbled.

'Ask her why she was using your phone!' Scott made one last effort to grab it before he went to sulk by the window.

'I'm not interested,' Dad said. 'All I want is a quiet life, OK? Tiffany, you ask in future before you ring your mates on my phone. And Scott, take Bud for a walk before he wrecks the place!'

Close! But I did it. At least, half of it. Now all I have to do is get Carli to say yes.

'Why not just persuade your dad to ask her out properly?' Geri asked me during lunch break.

Ellie had made a miraculous recovery and was noshing cheese and pickle sandwiches with the rest of us.

'Ah, you don't know Dad!' I explained. 'He's dead shy. And he's 38, remember. He was married for seventeen years, so he's most likely forgotten how to ask women out on dates.'

'I think it's dead romantic,' Shah sighed.

'Yeah, but how are you gonna get Miss Ganeri to turn up at that Italian place on Wednesday?' Geri asked.

'No problem,' I told them with a bright, breezy smile. 'She likes Dad. She'll show!'

Privately, I'm not so sure. I may have to throw in another little trick or two to get them together. But what? Wow, this match-making stuff is mega stressful! Will keep my fingers crossed that Carli texts Dad back with a Yes.

Spoke to Gran Little on the phone. Didn't mention U-Know-Wot!! She wanted to know if Dad had sweet-talked Mum into coming back yet. That's another Gran word – 'sweet-talked'.

'No, but Mum's buying me some boots this weekend,' I told her.

'Great, kiddo. Now put your father on the phone, will you.'

Poor dad got another ear bashing.

Talking of ears, I'm not happy. I looked in the mirror. They stick out more than I thought. Yikes, maybe they're growing!!! I need advice from my fave agony aunt.

Dear Claire,
How unlucky can you get? Not only are my breasts vanishing, but my ears are getting ginormous! Does God have it in for me, or what?'

Dear Tiffany,
God has nothing to do with it. It's all in your genes. And I'm not talking Levis. My advice is, stop worrying about little things. Remember, there arc millions of people worse off than you.

They are, they're growing! I used another mirror to look in my dressing-table mirror and saw

45

them from the back. It's horrible!!! Will try pinning them back with sellotape while I sleep. A girl can't go around looking like an elephant.

If it doesn't work, will DEFINITELY start saving up for plastic surgery!!!***!!!

## Tuesday, 6th February

 *Your stars* – *Don't plan too far ahead. Take each day as it comes.*

Sellotape left wrinkly lines on cheeks. Ears still flapping. Mum says I always exaggerate.

Resolution: must try to be sensible about ears. Aaagh!

Have decided to carry on with ghost story after all. I mean, it's a great, spooky idea; this skeleton trapped inside an ancient wall. And having one brother murder the other because they hate each others' guts (like, I could kill Scott sometimes!).

Gorgeous George took a look at it during English today. I didn't offer; he asked. So I dragged it out of the bottom of my bag. George blew off the bits of fluff and read it. 'D'you want to make it even more scary?' he asked. Then he suggested having bloodstains seeping through the ancient walls as a guide to where the body was buried. 'Not real blood,' he said. 'But a kind of strange, crimson vision, rising up like a tide!'

Ellie shivered and said, 'Yuck!'

Squealer sucked, then smacked his lips. 'Lovely jubbly!'

Will take George's advice. Must finish story and send it off to judges.

Slowly a deep red stain appeared on the stone wall. It oozed through the cracks and spread out across the floor. It rose towards the ceiling, bringing a wash of crimson to the whole room. And the ghostly voice whispered – outside, amongst the tall, bare trees, then through the window and into the ancient kitchen. 'Revenge!' it cried. 'I will have revenge!'

If I win first prize it'll prove George was right, that I do have a Special Talent. I mean, every kid in the country can enter this competition if they like. That's millions.

*'And the winner is . . . Ms Tiffany Little! Come on down, Tiffany! And let's give her a big round of applause!'*

I'll be famous, writing ghost stories for TV, making a film in Hollywood, meeting megastars!!

Dad hasn't mentioned his big date. Either he's playing it dead cool and not telling me about it, or Carli hasn't texted him back yet.

It must be that. I know Dad – if he'd got a mystery message on his phone, he'd be a bag of nerves. He'd be asking me what was going on, and I'd be spilling the beans about how I'd set him up, telling him to go ahead and have a good time. I'd be useless at keeping it quiet.

So, Miss Ganeri can't decide what to do. She likes Dad, but it turns out she's pretty shy too. Which means I still have to think of something to get them together, and fast! Hmmm.

Went round to Ellie's and found out what she's saving up for.

Not that it was easy.

'Go on, tell me!' We were messing about with lippies and eyeshadow in her room. Mr and Mrs Shelbourn were out at a tennis club thingy.

Ellie got a brush and painted a dark cupid's bow along her top lip. 'No, honestly Tiff, I'm not telling anyone!'

'Why not?'

'Cos!' She filled in with a paler colour, then pressed her lips together. 'Look, they're sealed!'

'What're you like!' Pretending not to care, I smudged Melted Honey on to my eyelids. According to the mags, with my dark colouring, I need to go for mellow golds and creams. Then I weakened. 'Oh go on, Ellie, I won't say anything!'

'No way!'

She was enjoying this, I could tell. 'Are you saving for new boots?' It was a wild guess, but worth a try.

'Nope.' Blusher on the cheeks, concealer on the tiny scar she had on her forehead from when she fell off the swing in the park.

'An electric guitar?' Another long shot, but then again Ellie was totally into music these days. Ever since she got chosen to sing in the school pop group, she hasn't thought of anything else.

'Nope.'

'What, then?' I knew I was whining, and I hated myself for it. I picked up her hairbrush and brushed my hair hard, so that it stuck up from the static electricity.

'D'you really wanna know?' Ellie said at last.

I felt like saying, no, don't bother, but she sailed on.

'I want to buy a ticket for the Savage Sister concert this Saturday.'

My mouth fell open. Tickets were £35 and anyway they were all sold out. 'No!'

'Yes! Mum knows someone at the tennis club who has a mate with a spare ticket, only she's refusing to buy it for me.'

'How come?' Now I was truly gobsmacked. Since when had Mrs S refused to give in to anything Ellie ever wanted?

'She doesn't like Savage Sister. She says they might give me the wrong idea about the type of singer I want to be.'

'Has she seen them?'

'Yeah, on Top of the Pops, yonks ago.' Ellie twisted her hair towards the back of her head and wound it into a silver clip.

'Basically she says I'm too young.'

'Hey, wait a minute!' I'd just thought of something. 'Saturday is my sleepover, remember!'

'Yeah, Tiff, which is very lucky when you think about it. I save up for Savage Sister and buy the ticket, but I tell Mum that I'm staying over at your place. Perfect!'

I frowned.

'Hey, Tiff, lighten up! I'm only asking you to cover for me if Mum happens to ask! You don't mind, do you?'

'But where will you really sleep?'

'Oh yeah, that's another thing.' Ellie smiled sweetly at me. 'Would your dad mind picking me up after the concert and bringing me back to your place? Then Mum won't suspect a thing!'

51

# Wednesday, 7th February

*Your stars* – You're not exactly a fan of the cold winter weather, so now's the time to splash out on some clothes in the mid-season Sales. Look for a bargain and you won't be let down.

Knee-length boots, here I come!

Scott hasn't talked to me for two days. If looks could kill, I'd be dead on the kitchen mat.

All because I wouldn't let on about the moby and Dad told him to walk Bud.

Actually, it's great, not having Scott on my back. In fact, I prefer it this way. It gives me more time to work out what to do about tonight. The Big Date. A New Start for Dad. The Beginning of all our Lives.

Dad will date Carli and they'll get on great. They'll see movies together, after a week or two she'll come back to our place and it'll be weird at first, having a teacher as Dad's girlfriend. But we'll soon get used to it – me, Bud and even Scott. After all, if Mum has Neil, Dad should have Carli. That's fair.

And the main thing is, Dad will be happy again.

This is how it'll happen: I'll go into school and find Miss Ganeri before assembly. She'll be in the Art Room, getting stuff ready for the day. I'll kind of drop a hint about Dad's text message, and say how he's really, really hoping she'll go out with him. She'll go red and awkward, then she'll smile and say yes, she'd been meaning to ring him back, and can I tell him she'll see him at Salvos at 7.30?

Well, you have to push and do stuff like that when the people are shy, like Dad and Carli.

It worked!

I did what I planned. Miss G gave me a funny look at first, but we got through that.

'Does your dad always ask you to set up his dates for him?' she asked, looking pretty mad actually.

I said no, he was just really nervous, and I wanted to help. Miss G guillotined a wodge of paper and let the scraps flutter to the floor. The sound of the sharp edge chomping through the sheets set my teeth on edge. 'What shall I tell him?' I pleaded.

She sliced through more paper, then nodded.

'Tell him I'll be there, 7.30 sharp.'

'But your dad still doesn't know!' Shah pointed out the major problem.

We were walking home from school, and Ellie had raced off to buy her Savage Sister ticket. (She'd scraped the cash together by borrowing from Geri and Shah. I'd given in over the Saturday night thing, but still had to work on Dad to agree to the sleep-over AND picking Ellie up.)

'That's true,' Geri realized. 'And it's supposed to be tonight, isn't it!'

'Yeah, no problem!' I was balancing

along the wall-top like a little kid, jumping gateways and ignoring the black looks.

'All I have to do now is slip him a little note that Miss G is supposed to have written, saying she'd like to meet up with him for a pizza, and how about tonight at 7.30?'

54

Shah gasped. 'Wow! You're gonna forge a note from Miss Ganeri?'

'Will he fall for it?' Geri wanted to know.

I jumped down from the wall. 'I bet you a million pounds!' I grinned. 'Just you wait, this is gonna turn out to be one of the most romantic first dates ever!'

Dad's dead easy to fool. I don't feel good saying that because it makes me sound sneaky, which I am sometimes. But only for a good cause. The thing about Dad is, he mostly believes what you tell him. He's always listening on the phone to sob stories from customers who can't pay their bills, and he says OK, leave it for another month, which is why we're eating stale cornflakes.

When I handed him 'Carli's' note – on the pale lilac, perfumed notepaper that Shah gave me at Christmas – he scratched his head.

'Where's this come from?' he mumbled.

'Miss Ganeri gave it to me to give to you.' (let's face it, that's SNEAKY!) 'Go on, open it!'

He fumbled for a bit. Then he read it. 'Bloo— bloomin' 'eck!'

'What's it say?' I asked, all sweet and innocent.

Bud had come up and started nosing at Dad, asking to be taken for a walk.

'She wants to go out with me,' Dad laughed.

'What's funny about that?' He had me worried for a second. 'You like her, don't you?'

'Hey, I only met her once.'

'Twice! And she's really nice. Not like a teacher at all!'

'Who's not?' Scott poked his nosey head around the door.

'Nobody. Scott, it's your turn to take Bud for a walk.' The reminder was guaranteed to get rid of him.

Scott vanished, beep-beeping away.

'Give her a call,' I urged Dad. 'Tell her that you'll be in the right place at the right time.'

(This wasn't as risky as it sounds, because I knew Miss G was in a staff meeting and her phone would be switched off. All Dad would need to do would be to leave a message.)

He dithered for ages – 'I don't know – I'm a bit nervous about this sort of thing – it's pretty short notice,' etcetera. But then he phoned and left the message; 'Hi, Carli. It's Ross Little here. 7.30 at Salvos, as arranged. See you there,' in a husky, embarrassed voice.

Then I hustled him upstairs into the shower.

Dad had one last try at escaping. 'What about Bud? Who's taking him?'

'I will!' I promised. That's how much I wanted this date to happen.

He showered and shaved, he brushed his teeth and came down looking like someone a thirty-something would want to go out with.

At seven o'clock I shoved him out of the door. 'Have a great time!' I yelled.

When I closed the door, Scott was lolling against the banister. He screwed up his mouth and eyes. 'If you've done what I think you've done, you're dead!' he warned.

'Naff off, Scott!'

'You've set him up on a date, haven't you?'

'What if I have? Get out of the way, I need the dog lead!'

He snatched it off the banister and held it behind his back.

'Who with?' he demanded.

'No one. Butt out. I mean it!' Scott's a lot taller

than me. He may look skinny and puny, but he can push me around when he wants. I have to use shock tactics to beat him. So I stamped on his foot, and as he bent double, I grabbed the lead.

Bud saw it and charged for the door. Woof!

The wind and rain blew in when I opened it. 'Dad's going out with Miss Ganeri, if you must know!' I called over my shoulder. 'He's gonna have fun for a change!'

I heard Scott groan and tell me I was dead for real this time. I slammed the door and headed out into the dark street. Rain splattered my face, the cracked pavement was shiny under the orange lights.

Disaster. Mega mega mistake!

It's twelve o'clock and I can hear Dad downstairs strumming his guitar. Bud is hiding under my bed until things get back to normal.

Dad went out at seven and was back by eight, white as a sheet.

'Don't ask!' he muttered, reaching for a beer. His hand was shaking as he turned on the TV.

My heart went thud, down into my trainers. Bud whined. Scott came stomping downstairs.

'Don't ask!' Dad groaned again.

The silence went on right through East-Enders.

Then the phone rang and I leaped to answer it.

'Tiffany?' Mum's voice came through loud and clear. 'What's going on over there?'

I grunted and swallowed hard.

Mum ranted on. 'I've just had a really weird phone call from your art teacher; she's accusing Ross of cheating on me by inviting her out on a date and stooping so low as to use you as a go-between!'

'Come again!' I squeaked.

'I said, Carli Ganeri is kicking up a storm about Ross asking her out behind my back! Apparently she got to the Italian place where they'd agreed to meet up, determined to teach him a lesson.'

'Oh!' I gasped. This time my heart was racing Formula 1 style.

'You might well say 'Oh!" Mum agreed. 'Ms Ganeri is a very determined lady. She even asked the school secretary for my mobile number! She arrives at Salvos, meets Ross and lets the waiter show them to their table. Your dad orders the wine, and half way through the first glass, totally out of the blue, she denounces him to the whole restaurant as a love-rat!'

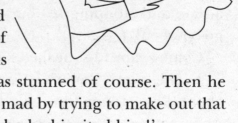

'Denounces?' I echoed.

'Yes, y'know; stands up in front of everybody and accuses him of cheating on his wife. Your dad was stunned of course. Then he made her doubly mad by trying to make out that she was the one who had invited him!'

'Oh!' I said again. Nightmare. My heart practically jumped out of my ribs!

'So Carli stormed out, went home and rang me. She said she thought I ought to know what my husband was up to. Well, I put her straight, told her the situation and said maybe next time she should check the school records before flinging mud all over the place. It says quite clearly that Ross and I are separated. She makes out she never read the record, or if she did it had slipped her mind, and anyway, hadn't she just seen us together at parents' evening?'

My mouth was dry, my hands were sweating, I couldn't think.

'Tiff?'

'Yeah, I'm still here.'

'I feel sorry for your dad, but you have to laugh, I s'pose. It was an honest mistake on her part. Can't you just imagine her standing up at the table and calling Ross horrible names!'

'Yeah,' I whispered. Too well. The picture sent me off on a massive guilt trip.

'And after he'd plucked up the courage to ask her out, poor Ross!'

I swallowed and tried to speak. 'Well, he didn't do that himself exactly.'

'What d'you mean? Tiffany, what's going on?'

Suddenly I had to fess up, or I'd burst.

'I did it,' I croaked. 'I set up the date. This whole mess is down to me!'

## Thursday, 8th February

*Your stars* – *It's like going back to nursery school later this week, as mates suck you into the name-calling and pony-tail pulling! Keep your cool and tell 'em to take a hike!*

'Oh, jeez!'

'Tiff, no!!'

'You never! She didn't! Oh wow!'

That was Geri, Shah and Ellie first thing this morning, when I met them in the cloakroom.

How lousy was I feeling?

'Never mind, eh?' Geri came across with the bright side. 'At least it gave the people in Salvos some free entertainment!' When I sighed, my ribcage still hurt from the pounding it got from my racing heart last night. Guilt feels like a heavy rock in my stomach.

'Watch out, here comes Miss Ganeri!' Ellie shrieked.

I jumped a mile and hid behind the lockers.

'Just kidding!' Ellie grinned.

'Tiff, try not to worry,' Shah advised. 'Worrying doesn't change anything. And anyway, I can see what you were aiming to do, and it was a nice idea.'

I sniffled and gulped.

Then Miss Hornby came and shunted us into the corridor. 'No wonder you four are always late for registration,' she grumbled; 'the amount of gossip that goes on in here!'

The whole day went on like that – me feeling bad about Dad, with Geri, Ellie and Shah doing their bit to cheer me up.

'It could be worse, Tiff,' Ellie said during English. 'At least your dad didn't ground you.'

'That's partly why I feel bad,' I whispered back. 'He hasn't told me off or anything, even when Mum told him the whole story. He just looks kind of sad and hurt.'

'Well anyway, at least Saturday's still on!'

Oh yeah, the sleepover.

'Did you ask your dad if he could pick me up after the concert?'

'Er – no, not yet.' My stomach churned.

'You promised!' Ellie hissed.

I nodded, felt sick and said I'd ask tonight.

Even Mr Fox handing back my latest piece of work and giving me an A didn't cheer me up. In fact, I felt much worse after he'd stopped by my desk.

'I hear you've been doing a spot of match-making!' he said with a smile.

Oh no! Now it was all around the staffroom, thanks to Miss Ganeri.

All the boys – Chucky, Marc, Squealer – stared at me.

'Nice effort, but from what I hear, the execution left something to be desired!' Gorgeous George moved on, leaving me feeling as if I'd been stabbed through the heart. Now he thinks I'm stupid and I'll never be able to talk to him or ask his advice about writing ever again!

That's it, I might as well give up. I'll work in a supermarket checkout or a petrol station. I'll burn my books.

'Cheer up, Tiff!' This was Dad when he got

home at teatime. I hate it that he acts normal after what I did.

'Have you got much homework?'

'Mega loads,' I lied. Then came up to the bedroom. Fiddled around filing my nails and trying out hairstyles. STUPID EARS!

Am horrible person. Don't need Scott's filthy looks to remind me. But he gives me them anyway.

Just before bed, am forced to go downstairs and ask Dad the favour for Ellie.

'Ellie wants me to pick her up after the Savage Sister concert?' He raised his eyebrows and looked hard at me.

I nodded. Please don't ask me if her mum knows!

'Does her mum know?' Dad quizzed.

Gulp. 'Dunno. 'Xpect so!'

'Hmm, OK. Sure, no problem.' Dad drifted off to find his guitar.

And I came up to bed.

# Friday, 9th February

Haven't bothered to look at stupid horoscope!!!

Black Friday.

First, Ellie came in late to registration, banging doors and flouncing around.

'Ah, Ellie, delighted to see you!' Miss H had her little joke.

'What's up?' Geri asked.

'I can't go to the concert on Saturday!' Ellie hissed.

'How come?' Shah and I gasped.

'Mum looked in my knicker drawer and found the ticket!' Her face was like thunder as Miss Hornby called the register.

'Here, Miss!' I croaked, then swivelled back to Ellie. 'How did she know?'

'Search me. It's just her nasty, suspicious mind, I expect.' Beneath the drama queen stuff, Ellie was genuinely upset. 'She's always sneaking around my room, tidying up and finding things. Now I'm banned from going and the ticket will be wasted. I'm not even allowed to play the latest Savage Sister CD!'

That made two of us with reasons to be seriously down.

Then, second thing: Shah told us at break that she was still grounded and couldn't come to the sleepover.

'I've been working on Mum and Dad to let me, but they say I've still got to catch up on my work. I *say* I've been doing homework till midnight every day this week, and they *say*, "Exactly; that's why you need early nights this weekend!"'

'Bummer!' Geri said. 'Parents!'

Third thing; Mum rang tonight and told me she couldn't take me shopping tomorrow.

'Something came up. I'm going to be away for a couple of days.'

I didn't even give her an argument. 'OK, no problem.'

'Are you all right, Tiff? You sound a bit down.'

A bit! 'I'm fine,' I sighed.

'Listen, darling, I'm sorry to let you down at the last moment. Tell you what, how about I bring over the money this evening and you go shopping with your mates instead?'

'Hey, thanks Mum!' Suddenly I perked up. Shopping magic!

'Will you be in?'

'Yeah.'

'What about your dad?'

'Out,' I told her. 'And Scott's watching telly.' Still not talking to me, but then, what's new?

I wrote a bit more of *The Voice* until Mum showed up. The modern day girl has seen the tide of blood rise up the old stone wall and has begun to take it apart. She chips away with a hammer and chisel until enough stones come free for her to crawl into the clammy, dark space behind. She shines a torch into the blackness:

Dreading each second, she felt her way forward. Then she stumbled. Her right foot had caught in something soft. Not stone. Not cobwebs. She shone the torch down at her feet. Her shoe was wrapped in a piece of cloth; a fragment of brown fabric which had mouldered there for years. There was a row of silver buttons along one edge, so it must have been part of a jacket.

Then shining the torch further into a dark corner, she stared down at what she had most dreaded. There was the dull white dome of a skull – the deep eye sockets, the grinning mouth – and beside it a crumbling heap of bones, scraps of leather with a buckle, the sole of a shoe turning to dust.

'Oh brother, I bleed!' a ghostly voice whispered. 'I bleed, I die! But still do not seal me inside this dreadful tomb!'

A key turned in the front door and made me jump. Then I realized it was Mum with the boots money, so I ran downstairs. She was standing in the hallway with Neil hovering on the doorstep behind. Mr Smarm-box gave me a sickly wave.

'What are you doing staying in all by yourself on a Friday night?' Mum asked after she'd hugged me.

I thought she was gonna turn into Gran Little and tweak my ears, the way she was going on. 'I'm not by myself. Scott's watching telly, remember!'

'Well, here's the cash.' she handed over a roll of notes, then a cheque. 'And this is for Ross. Tell him I'm sorry it's late.'

Phew, now we can buy Frosties! I said thanks and pinned the cheque to the kitchen notice-board.

Mum moved in closer, leaving Neil fidgeting by the front door. 'How is Ross after Wednesday's fiasco?' she murmured. 'Has he got over it yet?'

'Actually, yeah.' I was able to say this without lying. Dad hadn't exactly bounced back, but he had definitely smoothed over the whole thing – just one quiet, mopey guitar session, and that was it.

'I suppose the fact that he's out tonight is a good sign,' Mum decided. 'And you're sure you're OK?'

I put on a smile and said yes.

'Well, choose some good boots,' she said. 'Nothing too fancy. And some that you'll be able to walk in.' Hey, she *is* turning into Gran Little, just like I thought!

'Hi, Tiff!' Neil interrupted us with a tap on his watch. 'Have you seen the time, Gina?'

'Yeah, OK.' Mum stopped at the bottom of the stairs. 'Hi, Scott! Bye, Scott!'

He grunted back.

'See you, honey!' she grinned at me. Then they were gone.

## Saturday, 10th February

 *Your stars* – Maybe it's the dark mornings, but just lately you seem to be suctioned to your bed. Wake up to your fave Latino number and salsa your way thru the day!

Well, I was up and salsa-ing at half-seven, thanks. Today it's Shop Till We Drop!!!

Geri, Ellie and Shah got to my house by nine. We swapped tops and borrowed shoes. Ellie and I are the same size for everything. Shah did Geri's hair. Geri's hockey match was cancelled because of the frost, otherwise she wouldn't have been here. Honest, she'd rather play Centre Forward for Ashbrook Firsts than hang with the gang – weird!

'Wrap up warm, kiddos!' That was Gran, who just happened to have dropped by, complete with weekend bag. 'You three need looking after!' she'd announced. 'And this house could do with a woman's touch!'

Dad never argues with Gran. 'Fine by me,' he'd told her. 'Only, be warned. I've agreed to let a gaggle of giggling girls sleep over in Tiff's room tonight!'

'I'd better get baking,' Gran had said.

By half-ten, Geri, Shah, Ellie and me had been in Top Shop, River Island and Miss Selfridge. We'd tried on all the boots in town.

High-heeled boots, like this:

72

Knee-length boots, like this:

Boots with stiletto heels, like this:

'I thought you were s'posed to buy something sensible,' Geri reminded me.

'Boring!' Ellie said, seizing the flashiest boots there – red leather with swirls of silver studs. 'Try this.'

'What about the heels?' Shah saved me from the red leather and kept me on track.

I was hot and sticky, my feet were killing me, but I shopped on. I definitely didn't want anything coloured. In fact, my dream boots were black, knee-length, with heels I could walk in, and definitely no studs.

The only problem was, I hadn't found the exact thing so far. We were out on the street, spread out across the pavement, bumping into lamp posts, laughing and chilling. I was catching my breath after the last ten pairs I'd tried in Miss S, when suddenly Ellie said, 'Hey, Harvey Nicks!' and took a quick left past a fat man in a coat, hat and white gloves.

'Errk!' Geri rolled her eyes and braked hard.

'You have to pay to breathe in there!' Shah whispered.

'Come back!' I mouthed at Ellie through the glass door, while the guy in the hat frowned hard.

She ignored us and sailed on into the store.

We three took deep breaths and bumbled in after her.

'Did you see the look the doorman gave us?' Shah muttered.

The smell of perfume hit us like a warm blast. We sank into the deep carpet. Women with make-up and long nails stared at us from behind the counters.

'Cool!' Ellie waited for us at the foot of the escalator. It was like she'd died and gone to designer-label heaven.

'I can't afford anything in here!' I squeaked.

The escalator hummed, we rose through clouds of Tommy Girl.

'Natch,' Ellie breezed. 'But you look in here for something you really really like, then we go out and find a cheap copy!'

'Cool!' Shah and Geri agreed with the shopping expert. Yeah, but they didn't have to try on the boots for £500, with the snooty assistant keeping her beady eye on us.

Ellie had picked out some black, knee-length boots, and Shah and Geri had crowded into the cubicle with me. I was looking at myself in the long mirror, when suddenly Ellie slid back the curtain.

'Tiff, you're not gonna believe this!' she gasped.

'What?' It was getting stuffy in there with four of us. I was crushed against the mirror.

'I've just spotted Miss Ganeri in the shoe section!'

'Is that all?' Geri shoved with her elbows. 'I thought it was something mega important!'

'It is!' I hissed. The 500 quid boots were getting creased, but no way did I want to bump into Miss G. I hadn't seen her since Wednesday, and I planned to keep it that way.

'No, it really, really is!' Ellie was fizzing and fussing.

'You're never gonna believe this, but our art teacher is trying on shoes with Gabi!'

'Gabi who?' Geri was still wrestling her way to freedom. I got an elbow in my back and stumbled sideways.

'Gabi Moss from Savage Sister!' Ellie found a pen and a scrap of paper in the bottom of her bag.

'You're kidding me!' Shah pushed past to break out of the cubicle. She took a quick look and reported back. 'It's true!' she hissed.

So we all staggered free and the disgusted assistant snatched the boots from my hands.

'See!' Ellie said, standing almost speechless for once. I stared across a forest of racks and display stands, and yeah, there was a woman with long,

blonde hair and dark glasses, dressed in a micro skirt and tight leopard-skin top, trying on long, black, spiky-heeled boots.

'Isn't she cool?' Ellie breathed. There were stars in her eyes, blinding her to whatever else was going on around.

'So where's Miss Ganeri?' I asked.

'Never mind that, I want Gabi's autograph!' Ellie clicked into action, darting between the rails, on the scent of a celeb. In her hurry, she bashed against a dummy in a strappy silver evening dress and sent it flying. Three assistants came running.

'Uh-oh!' Geri pulled a face, then decided to join in.

Shah and I watched Gabi Moss turn towards Ellie and Geri, one boot on and one boot off. She looked around for help, but if Miss Ganeri had ever been there with her, she wasn't any longer.

By now, other customers were drifting towards the action and a small crowd was gathering. The three assistants had rescued the toppled dummy and one had called Security.

Ellie reached Shoes and stopped. She clutched her scrap of paper, dumbstruck. The superstar stooped to pull on the other boot.

'P-p-please, c-c-could I have your autograph?' Ellie stammered.

Sidling around the silver dummy and three assistants, I saw Mr Muscles in a dark suit glide silently up the escalator. Ms Glamour tutted and sighed. 'This is forever happening to me!'

'Gabi, please!' Ellie approached with her pen and paper. 'I'm your number one fan!'

The blonde swatted her away. 'You're out of luck, I'm afraid.' She turned to the mirror to study the boots.

'B-but . . .!' Ellie's top lip was trembling. The shooting star was tumbling to earth.

'I'm not who you think I am, OK!'

'Not Gabi?'

'Uh-oh!' Geri said again, as Shah and I reached them.

The Suit was striding towards us. The crowd was drifting away.

'Definitely not!' the Gabi lookalike insisted. 'People always make that mistake. But no, I'm just bog-ordinary Michelle Palmer from Hunter's Heath, trying my best to buy a pair of boots!'

When we got kicked out of Harvey Nicks by The Suit, The Uniform at the Door eyeballed us and sneered.

'Bummer!' Geri said.

No boots and no autograph. And Ellie was feeling about two centimetres high. 'I was sure that was Gabi!' she sighed.

For a second, I thought she was about to go back in and double-check. I grabbed her arm. 'You say you saw Ganeri with her?'

Ellie nodded.

'Well, get real: no way would Gabi be hanging out with a teacher from our school!'

'Yeah!' Geri and Shah backed me up.

'Well, maybe I was wrong about Ganeri,' Ellie admitted. 'But I was right about Gabi, I know it!'

So we hung about for ages at the door of

Harvey Nicks, waiting for the Savage Sister to come out.

'Maybe she left by the back door,' Shah said after half an hour.

'Maybe she really was Michelle Wotsit from Wotsit Heath,' I added. My feet were like blocks of ice, and I still didn't have any boots.

'Let's go!' Geri decided.

We shopped some more and forgot about the Gabi Ross incident, all except Ellie. Her mind still wasn't on zip or buttons, leather or suede. She didn't even bother when we swooped through Accessorize. Sparkly scrunchies couldn't tempt her, nor even six funky neon pink bracelets for 99p.

We had fries in McDonalds at one, and I'd found my dream boots by three. Marathon, or what?

*Saturday evening.*

\* \* \* \* \*
### SURPRISE SATURDAY! GOBSMACKING, UNBELIEVABLE, SUPER-COOL SATURDAY!
\* \* \* \* \*

'Enjoy!' Gran ordered.

While we were out shopping, she'd baked and baked. Now everyone was at my house for the sleepover and we were tucking in to home-made doughnuts and choccy biscuits.

'Shah, how come your mum and dad said yes?' Geri mumbled through a mouthful of sugary doughnut. The jam splurged out and dribbled down her chin.

'Tiff's dad rang up specially and asked if I could come.'

Which was news to me. But thanks, Dad!

Ellie's mum had dropped both Ellie and Shah off, had chatted quietly with Dad, then shot off in her four-wheel drive. Dad had gone upstairs for a shower and Gran had given us tea.

*'So what? So, what's new?*
*Tell me the things I wanna hear*
*Like I – lurve – you!'*

81

That was Dad singing a Savage Sister song in the shower. We giggled and spluttered choccy crumbs across the table.

'He's in a good mood,' Shah said.

'Yeah, I don't get it.' I shook my head. Ever since Thursday he'd been going around whistling and singing.

Gran listened, her head to one side, sniffing hard. 'I smell aftershave. He must be going out.'

We munched away, planning the evening. Geri had brought Magic 8 Ball and Scrabble. Shah wanted to use the make-up kit she'd bought earlier, and Ellie was into being a disco diva with her new karaoke system.

*'So hey! Tell it to me straight*
*Is this lurve or is it hate?'*

Dad warbled from the bathroom to his bedroom. We jumped up and joined in the chorus, doing Savage Sister hand movements and dancing along.

*'Tell it to me, tell it to me*
*Give it to me straight!'*

'Very nice, kiddos,' Gran mumbled, clearing the table and going to answer the doorbell.

*'Tell me the things I wanna hear,*
*You and me, babe!'*

'Ross!' Gran shouted upstairs. 'There's a woman at the door!' Scott shot out of his room and peered over the banister.

Geri, Ellie, Shah and me put our heads round the kitchen door. And there stood Miss Ganeri!

Miss G in a short skirt and ankle boots. Carli in her purple and black going-out top, wearing dark red lipstick.

I ducked back into the kitchen and held my

breath. Oh no, not again! Wednesday night had come back to haunt me, like the dead brother in *The Voice*!

Dad clomped downstairs, no doubt ready to take more flak. It looked like Miss G hadn't gotten over Salvos yet. I was still not breathing, praying for her to fade into the night.

'Hi, Ross!'

'Hi, Carli!'

I heard two 'Mwahs!' and a kiss on the cheek.

What? I crept to the door and peered out.

'Ready?' Carli asked with a big red smile. She held up a blue ticket for Dad to see.

'Ready!' he held up one of his own. His hair was smart, his chin was smooth, and he was dressed in a NEW SUEDE JACKET!!!

'How d'you like my boots?' Carli asked him, holding one leg up. 'They're new. They cost me an arm and a . . .'

'Leg!' he grinned. Then,

'What about this jacket?'

She stroked his arm. 'Smooth!'

Scott disappeared and slammed his door.

The four of us went on gawping.

'Come in, er – Carli. Don't stand in the cold,' Gran insisted.

'It's OK, Mum, we're off out to a concert,' Dad told her.

'We might be late, so don't wait up.'

'We'? 'Concert'?!!!

'Hey, how did you get those?' Ellie sprang out into the hallway. 'They're Savage Sister tickets, aren't they?'

Miss G smiled. 'Yeah, they're like gold dust. But it just so happens – well, let's say I have friends in high places!'

Shah, Geri and me came forward open mouthed.

'Who?' Ellie demanded.

By now Carli was grinning. 'Gabi Ross and I went to art college together,' she confessed. 'We go way back to before she was famous!'

There was this massive silence.

'It *was* her!' Ellie almost blubbed. 'In Harvey Nicks – you and her – buying shoes!'

'Guilty!' Carli admitted. 'I'd gone off to look

at make-up, but Gabi told me all about the four girls and the shop dummy, and the way she'd fobbed you off to avoid a riot. She was afraid the whole store would go hysterical, so she had to tell a little white lie. Hey, I might have guessed the star-struck blonde kid would turn out to be you, Ellie!'

'I knew it was Gabi all along!' Ellie wailed.

But personally, I had other stuff to sort out with Dad. 'Hey!' I got through the crush and tugged at his sleeve. 'How come you have a ticket?'

He pulled his cuff free and smoothed the suede. 'From Vanessa.'

'Ellie's Mum?' I remembered the cosy chat when Mrs Shelbourn dropped Ellie and Shah off.

'That's *my* ticket!' Ellie cried.

I grabbed Dad again and pulled harder this time, all the way back into the kitchen. 'And what about you and her?' I hissed, stabbing my finger towards the hallway. 'Last I heard, she was chucking wine over you in Salvos!'

'Don't get carried away,' Dad warned. 'There was never any wine involved.'

'You know what I mean. You two had that massive row, so how come now you're dating all of a sudden?'

'Why not? Wasn't this your idea in the first place!'

'Dad, tell me!'

'OK!' He was worried about his precious jacket, so he had to give in. 'On Thursday, once I'd got over the shock of Salvos, I gave Carli a call to say I was sorry about the shambles of the night before. She said maybe she shouldn't have jumped to conclusions, then we had a good laugh about the whole thing and I asked her out again.'

'And she said yes!' Wow! I mean, wow, the best! My face must've lit up like Christmas lights.

'OK by you?' Dad checked.

I nodded. I couldn't say anything, I was too gobsmacked.

So Carli and Dad went to the Savage Sister concert. Gran warned them to wrap up well. 'They forecast frost,' she said.

I could tell she wasn't happy, the way she tutted and went on about wearing vests to avoid catching a cold after they'd gone.

Neither was Scott, but then what's new?

Me, Shah, Geri and Ellie ignored the two misery guts and played Magic 8 Ball.

'Carli promised to get me Gabi's autograph!' Ellie told us, before she switched on the karaoke machine and we discoed the night away.

## Sunday, 11th February

*Your stars* – At long last, a kiss that's been on the cards for ages looks as though it's about to happen – lucky you!

Dad is Gemini. 'Nuff said.

We slept in. Gran brought us breakfast in my room. Dad was outside washing his van, whistling.

'Anyone awake up there?' I heard the front door open and Dad's voice yelling.

'Uu-uuh!' I had one eye half open, the sun was streaming in through the crack in the curtains.

'You've got visitors!'

'Mmmmm!'

'Shall I tell them to go away again?'

'Who is it?' I staggered out of bed and crept on to the landing. I blinked, rubbed my eyes and blinked again. 'Ellie, Shah, Geri, come here quick!'

I waited for what seemed like a century, while Carli stood waving from the hallway, next to – yeah, next to Gabi Ross!

'Hi, girls!' Gabi smiled and waved at the four mop-heads who appeared at the top of the stairs.

'Surprise!' Carli laughed. 'Hey, if you can't get along to the concert, this has to be the next best thing!'

It turned out that Gabi was cool. None of the I-am-a-star stuff. She may have been top of the pops for the last ten years, but behind the dark glasses, when you get her in an ordinary house, chilling with a smelly dog and a room full of normal people, she's just like anyone else. She laughed at Dad's jokes and giggled when Carli reminded her of stuff they'd done at college.

After a while, I dashed upstairs and dug out my

autograph book. Gabi signed it four times
– one for each of us.

'What d'you wanna do
when you're older?' she
asked us.

'Play sport for England,'
Geri said.

'Go to art college,' from
Shah.

'Sing in a band,' was Ellie's answer.

'Be a famous writer,' was mine.

Gabi wrote me a message:

> *To Tiffany,*
> *May all your dreams come true!*
> *Love from Gabi*
>
> *xxx*

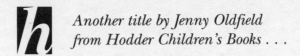

*Another title by Jenny Oldfield
from Hodder Children's Books . . .*

# Definitely Daisy 1
# You're a disgrace, Daisy!

Meet Daisy Morelli – a magnet
for trouble and a master plotter.
When things go wrong – and they
always do – who gets the blame?
Definitely Daisy!

Daisy's fed up with school, so
she plans to run away – chucking
in boring lessons for footballing
stardom! If only the junior
Soccer Academy will have her . . .